INDIANAPOLIS COLTS

BY TOM GLAVE

The Child's World®

Published by The Child's World®
1980 Lookout Drive • Mankato, MN 56003-1705
800-599-READ • www.childsworld.com

Acknowledgments
The Child's World®: Mary Berendes, Publishing Director
Red Line Editorial: Editorial direction
The Design Lab: Design
Amnet: Production

Design Element: Dean Bertoncelj/Shutterstock Images
Photographs ©: Gene J. Puskar/AP Images, cover;
Thomas E. Witte/Icon Sportswire, 5; Bettmann/Corbis,
7; Michael Conroy/AP Images, 9; Charles Krupa/AP
Images, 11; Alexey Stiop/Shutterstock, 13; Scott Boehm/
AP Images, 14–15; Cliff Welch/Icon Sportswire, 17; Aaron
M. Sprecher/AP Images, 19; Joe Robbins/AP Images,
21; Larry W. Smith/Icon Sportswire, 23; MSA/Icon
Sportswire, 25; Rich Kane/Icon Sportswire, 27; Kevin
Terrell/AP Images, 29

ISBN 9781631439964
LCCN 2014959701

Printed in the United States of America
Mankato, MN
July, 2015
PA02265

ABOUT THE AUTHOR

Tom Glave grew up watching football on TV and playing it in the field next to his house. He learned to write about sports at the University of Missouri–Columbia and has written for newspapers in New Jersey, Missouri, Arkansas, and Texas. He lives near Houston, Texas, and cannot wait to play backyard football with his kids Tommy, Lucas, and Allison.

TABLE OF CONTENTS

GO, COLTS!

The Indianapolis Colts franchise started in 1953. Their first home was in Baltimore, Maryland. They moved to Indianapolis in 1984. Baltimore fans were upset. But fans in Indianapolis were happy to get the team. They have seen some great players. First they rooted for Peyton Manning. He is one of the best quarterbacks ever. Now they get to watch star quarterback Andrew Luck. Let's meet the Colts.

Peyton Manning (18), one of the best quarterbacks of all time, led the Colts to the Super Bowl after the 2006 season.

4

WHO ARE THE COLTS?

The Indianapolis Colts play in the National Football **League** (NFL). They are one of the 32 teams in the NFL. The NFL includes the American Football Conference (AFC) and the National Football Conference (NFC). The winner of the AFC plays the winner of the NFC in the **Super Bowl**. The Colts play in the South Division of the AFC. They have played in the Super Bowl four times. They won after the 1970 and 2006 seasons. They also won two NFL Championships before the Super Bowl began after the 1966 season.

Teammates celebrate with legendary quarterback Johnny Unitas (19) after winning the 1959 NFL Championship.

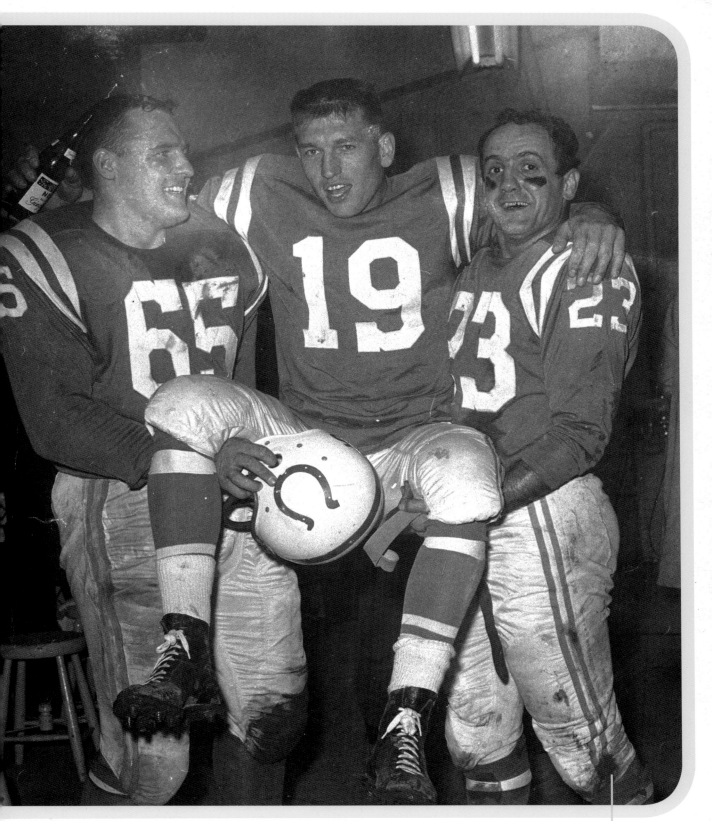

WHERE THEY CAME FROM

Baltimore got an NFL team in 1953. It was named the Colts. They had many great years in Baltimore. But owner Robert Irsay was not happy. He wanted a nicer stadium. Irsay also did not think fans cared enough. So he moved the Colts to Indianapolis on March 28, 1984. Irsay hired a moving company. It moved the team overnight. Football fans in Indianapolis were excited. The team had 143,000 season ticket requests in two weeks. Indianapolis drafted quarterback Peyton Manning in 1998. The Colts have been one of the best teams in the NFL ever since.

The Colts finished their rough first season in Indianapolis with a 4–12 record.

WHO THEY PLAY

The Indianapolis Colts play 16 games each season. With so few games, each one is important. Every year, the Colts play two games against each of the other three teams in their division. Those teams are the Tennessee Titans, Houston Texans, and Jacksonville Jaguars. The Colts also play six other teams from the AFC and four from the NFC. Indianapolis and the New England Patriots are rivals. The rivalry started when both teams were good in the 2000s. Quarterbacks Peyton Manning and Tom Brady had many memorable duels.

Indianapolis games against the New England Patriots were must-see TV when Peyton Manning and Tom Brady went head to head.

WHERE THEY PLAY

The Colts first played in the Hoosier Dome in Indianapolis. It was later named the RCA Dome. Now the Colts call Lucas Oil Stadium home. It opened in 2008. It is one of three NFL stadiums with a retractable roof. Its roof is the only one that opens from sideline to sideline. The stadium can hold 67,000 fans. It hosted the Super Bowl after the 2011 season. It is also used for college basketball and football games.

The Colts have scored a lot of points in Lucas Oil Stadium since it opened in 2008.

THE FOOTBALL FIELD

MIDFIELD

BENCH AREA

20-YARD LINE

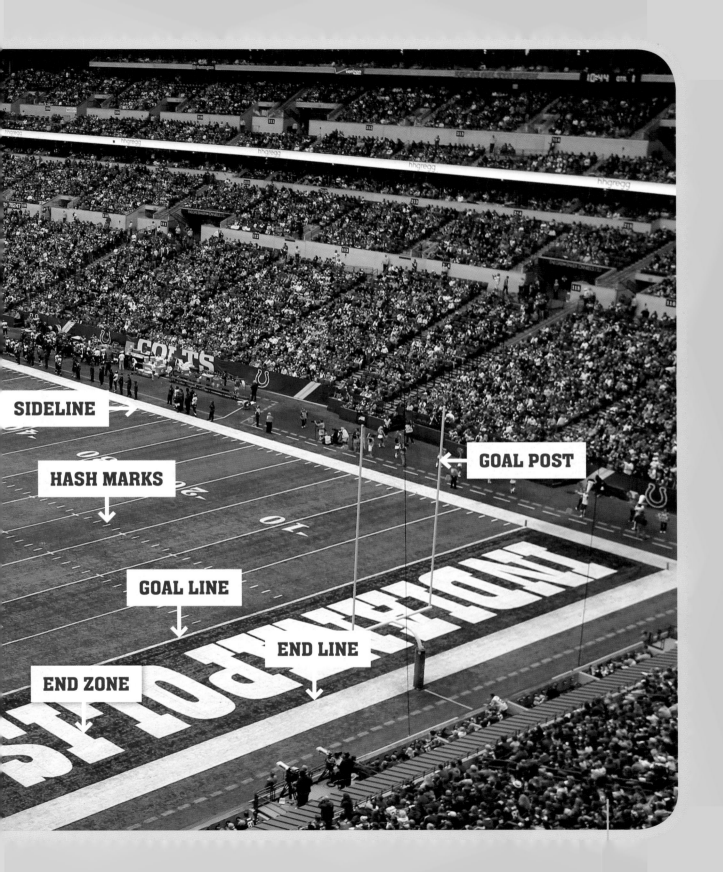

SIDELINE

HASH MARKS

GOAL POST

GOAL LINE

END LINE

END ZONE

BIG DAYS

The Colts have had some great moments in their history. Here are three of the greatest:

1958—The Colts won their first NFL Championship. They beat the New York Giants 23-17 on December 28. Quarterback Johnny Unitas led two late drives for the win. It was the first NFL Championship Game to go into **overtime**. It has been called "The Greatest Game Ever Played."

2006—The Colts won their first Super Bowl in Indianapolis. They beat the Chicago Bears 29-17 on February 4, 2007. Defensive back Kelvin Hayden returned an interception for a touchdown in the fourth quarter. That sealed the win.

Colts fans were sad to see Peyton Manning go but excited the team selected Andrew Luck (right) in the 2012 NFL Draft.

2012—Quarterback Peyton Manning left the Colts. He joined the Denver Broncos. Colts fans were worried. But the team drafted quarterback Andrew Luck on April 26. He quickly became one of the best quarterbacks in the NFL. The Colts were once again in good hands.

TOUGH DAYS

Football is a hard game. Even the best teams have rough games and seasons. Here are some of the toughest times in Colts history:

1981—The Colts lost 14 straight games. It is still their longest losing streak. They allowed the most points in the NFL. It was one of six straight losing seasons before the team moved to Indianapolis.

1991—Quarterback Jeff George was supposed to be great. But Indianapolis went 14-35 in his four seasons there. This season was the worst. The Colts had the NFL's worst offense. They did not score a **touchdown** in five straight games. Indianapolis finished 1-15.

New Orleans Saints running back Pierre Thomas (23) runs with the ball during his team's 62-7 win over the Colts on October 23, 2011.

2011—Peyton Manning could not play after having neck surgery. The Colts went 2-14 without him. They lost their first 13 games. The worst was a 62-7 defeat to the New Orleans Saints. Manning joined the Denver Broncos in 2012. An era ended.

MEET THE FANS

Indianapolis fans are some of the best in the NFL. The Colts inducted them into the team's Ring of Honor in 2007. Fans wear blue and white to games. Those are the team colors. There are pregame parties outside the stadium. Fans play games and listen to music. They also have fun with mascot Blue. He is a blue horse that wears a white jersey.

Blue has been the Colts' official mascot since 2006.

HEROES THEN

Johnny Unitas was the Colts' quarterback from 1956 to 1972. He was great under pressure. Unitas set an NFL record of 47 straight games with a touchdown pass. He often threw to wide receiver Raymond Berry. Berry led the NFL in receptions for three straight seasons. Tight end John Mackey also played with Unitas. He was a strong blocker and good receiver. Quarterback Peyton Manning is another Colts legend. He was the NFL's **Most Valuable Player** four times with Indianapolis. Wide receivers Marvin Harrison and Reggie Wayne had great connections with Manning.

Wide receiver Marvin Harrison made eight straight Pro Bowls from 1999 to 2006.

HEROES NOW

The Colts chose Andrew Luck first in the 2012 NFL Draft. Indianapolis made the playoffs in his first three seasons. He set the NFL **rookie** record with 4,374 passing yards in 2012. T. Y. Hilton is carrying on the tradition of great Colts receivers. He is small but quick. He made his first Pro Bowl in 2014. Defender Robert Mathis led the NFL with 19.5 **sacks** in 2013. He was named to five Pro Bowls from 2008 to 2013.

Defensive end Robert Mathis tackles quarterback Alex Smith in a playoff game against the Kansas City Chiefs on January 4, 2014.

GEARING UP

NFL players wear team uniforms. They wear helmets and pads to keep them safe. Cleats help them make quick moves and run fast. Some players wear extra gear for protection.

THE FOOTBALL

NFL footballs are made of leather. Under the leather is a lining that fills with air to give the ball its shape. The leather has bumps or "pebbles." These help players grip the ball. Laces help players control their throws. Footballs are also called "pigskins" because some of the first balls were made from pig bladders. Today they are made of leather from cows.

Wide receiver Reggie Wayne led the NFL with 1,510 receiving yards in 2007.

HELMET

SHOULDER PADS

GLOVES

THIGH PADS

FOOTBALL

CLEATS

SPORTS STATS

Here are some of the all-time career records for the Indianapolis Colts. All the stats are through the 2014 season.

PASSING YARDS

Peyton Manning 54,828

Johnny Unitas 39,768

INTERCEPTIONS

Bobby Boyd 57

Don Shinnick 37

RECEPTIONS

Marvin Harrison 1,102

Reggie Wayne 1,070

TOTAL TOUCHDOWNS

Marvin Harrison 128

Lenny Moore 113

SACKS

Robert Mathis 111

Dwight Freeney 107.5

POINTS

Mike Vanderjagt 995

Adam Vinatieri 988

Running back Edgerrin James led the NFL in rushing yards in 1999 and 2000, his first two years in the league.

RUSHING YARDS

Edgerrin James 9,226

Lydell Mitchell 5,487

GLOSSARY

league an organization of sports teams that compete against each other

Most Valuable Player a yearly award given to the top player in the NFL

overtime extra time that is played when teams are tied at the end of four quarters

rivals teams whose games bring out the greatest emotion between the players and the fans on both sides

rookie a player playing in his first season

sacks when the quarterback is tackled behind the line of scrimmage before he can throw the ball

Super Bowl the championship game of the NFL, played between the winners of the AFC and the NFC

touchdown a play in which the ball is held in the other team's end zone, resulting in six points

FIND OUT MORE

IN THE LIBRARY

Gigliotti, Jim. *Super Bowl Super Teams.*
New York: Scholastic, 2010.

Nagelhout, Ryan. *Peyton Manning.*
New York: Gareth Stevens Publishing, 2014.

Stewart, Mark. *The Indianapolis Colts.*
Chicago: Norwood House, 2013.

ON THE WEB

Visit our Web site for links about the Indianapolis Colts:
childsworld.com/links

Note to Parents, Teachers, and Librarians: We routinely verify our Web links to make sure they are safe and active sites. So encourage your readers to check them out!

INDEX